About the Author

John Girdwood was born in 1964 and has resided in Wester Hailes, Edinburgh his entire life. A father of two, a son and a daughter, and also a grandfather for the last eighteen months. Due to ill health, John had to retire from a successful career in the hospitality industry and to pick up writing in his spare time, purely as a hobby. After positive feedback from friends, John submitted his first manuscript to Austin Macauley, in the fantasy genre, and is proud to present his finished work in this book.

Dedication

"In loving memory of my mother,

Mary Johnston Campbell Girdwood.

Never forgotten,

In the arms of the Lord God.

John Girdwood

FLATWORLD2^

AUSTIN MACAULEY PUBLISHERS™

LONDON · CAMBRIDGE · NEW YORK · SHARJAH

A CIP catalogue record for this title is available from the British Library.

ISBN 9781035825738 (Paperback)
ISBN9781035825745 (ePub e-book)

www.austinmacauley.com

First Published 2024
Austin Macauley Publishers Ltd®
1 Canada Square
Canary Wharf
London
E14 5AA

Acknowledgements

I would like to thank the following people for their unwavering support:

Kevin Henderson for his technical help

My taxi friends—they know who they are

Joe and Jess and Jack

Michelle for being there

The Multiverse. It is all that there is, all that there ever has been, and all that there will ever be. It is everything of balance and it is everything of opposition. It is where time and space simultaneously travel in equal and opposite direction. Where everything is united and also divided. And essentially, for every force and every energy expenditure everywhere, then somewhere there must be an equal and identical reaction to neutralise it.

(FlatWorld),

War and battle seemed to have perpetually raged on the FlatWorld, a dwelling that, like all Worlds where strife was common, felt grim and monotonous. It was a pre-industrial society and could be described as being civilised if a constant state warfare didn't exist between its peoples. It was fairly large, covering an area approximately twice the size of the continent of Europe on the Multiverse dwelling named Earth. It was a world of opposition and division however. A proud LightSide, pitted against a dark grey side, desired to extinguish the glad brightness the light radiated. The shine itself was a fierce and unforgiving force that wished nothing less than the total dispersal of the shadow. Seeking a peaceful balance of such forces and to find settlement, to even gain the slightest glimpse of the displayed wonder contained within a stable fusion of both the dark and the light, has been considered unattainable for more than 6000 years.

Despite numerous similarities between all the peoples, it was most unfortunate that the situation existed between the two opposing forces inhabiting the green and fertile lands of the FlatWorld. There was the white kingdom and the GreySide Realm, both comprising a variety of peoples from Royal Houses and hardy Farmers to Legions of Men astride flying Beasts. There were Waarg-Masters also, and vicious GoblOrcs of savage abilities, and row on row of grim-faced Infantry, wielding forged-steel. There were some sorts of creative arts and a degree of free thinking amongst the populations, although these were concentrated primarily within the royal courts. The main production output of FlatWorld was involved with and focused on warfare, which was sad as it was a very beautiful world.

Its long lush green fields were intricately woven and laced by sparkling, clean waterways, large and small, seeking the distant oceans. And skirting the bases of imposing mountain ranges there was spread enormous swathes of dense woodlands which bordered the deepest of blue lakes, teeming with water life of dizzying array. Even those only hinted at the beauty of the lands they were a part of, with enormous tracts of largely unspoiled areas supporting a proliferation of various creatures and thick green pastures were stocked full with many farm animals and fatted calves.

Despite it being a mature landscape long inhabited by peoples, almost no written documents existed attesting to the history and age of the ands. Endless conflict dictated that children grew up with sword and shield rather than chalk and papyrus. The only way that deeds were remembered was when recalled in songs and precious little heed was paid to dates when there abounded great feats of strength and victory in battle. The two civilisations living on the FlatWorld were both of proud bearing. Unfortunately the distrust between one another ensured that when they were not actively engaged in outright warfare, then they were both diligently working on replenishment and replacement. If ever a peace could be brokered between the two factions, there is little doubt that FlatWorld would be as close to utopian as was possible to get.

Old wives however did speak down the countless generations of the legend of permanent-peace, a strange tale that insisted there would come one day, a dry and rainless thunderstorm of frightening fury and voice heard all over the FlatWorld. And thereafter would appear in the sky another sun, named QuietLight, which would remain visible until peace was won or lost. All on FlatWorld knew the legend as it was oft related via bedtime stories for young children or even drunken debate in the Alehouses. It was known best by royalty. The opposing royal houses had deep respect for the legend. Unbeknown to all but very few, they both had in their possession ancient and fragile scraps of parchment-paper, adorned with symbols which appeared to relate directly to the legendary signs foretelling lasting peace.

It was long-known by the royal scribes of both kingdoms that they each had missing pieces. However the losses had come to pass over the ages, it rendered both sets incomplete and therefore of little use. These scrolls put together could, possibly, offer a path for the Pure-blooded to lead their FlatWorld into a peaceful and happy golden age. Sadly, hate and suspicion for each other prevailed, so no thought of this, or conference for any reason had entered any King or Generals mind in living or indeed even dead memory.

Unaware of the fragile scraps of parchment-paper, no-one else of senior influence in the two kingdoms paid much attention to the legend of peace, considering it nothing more than a strong propaganda tool amid their arsenal of weaponry, and a story for the workers and front line soldiers to pin their own personal wishes to, providing them with another reason to fight. Hope. The emotion that had ever been essential for the masses to cling on to. Such a simple thing but wielding the power to move mountains. And with careful manipulation of the ears that heard whispered rumour of victory assured, hope could be used as the sharpest of all weapons of war.

(Edinburgh),

James Mackenzie and his wife Marianne were known by everyone as Mac and Mari' and had been since meeting at the world renowned Heriot-Watt University of Edinburgh. They had married before graduation and devoted themselves to their careers. The hoped-for and desired parenthood, never happened, and now aged 40 and 39 years old, Mac and Mari' were as much in love with each other as when they first met. They were a pragmatic couple and had taken the fact that they were likely to remain childless in their stride, accepting the "you can't have it all" approach which had served them well in previous years. They shared many passions together and ran an exclusive antique shop in Edinburgh's wealthy Stockbridge area. They had both achieved their degrees in Ancient Artifacts and Dialects, achieving 'Firsts' with relative ease. Archaeological categorising and the relative histories were interesting 'side-hobbies', which the pair of them loved studying. The fact that they were childless allowed them to travel extensively to the far East and Asia mostly, an area of the world they loved the many mystical sides of.

Respected colleagues, dignitaries or even just simply curious locals from as far away as the Russian Steppes to the South of Iran and even to a wide variety of regional areas of China were always impressed, with some of the older and most-respected families being honoured by their abilities in linguistics and the sheer depths of knowledge they had on whichever area they visited and they forged many friendships wherever they went. They were always welcomed with genuine warmth when they returned to previously visited cities, towns and indeed villages, some of which were extremely remote, accessible only by small river-boats, bestowing an almost magical quality upon them.

When they were so secluded, so far from the white-noise of bustling cities or hurried market-towns, Mac and Mari' loved ending their days playing Backgammon, or more often Chess, in the beautifully coloured and warm, balmy evening sunsets that bore little resemblance to the damp, cold 5 pm darkness of Edinburgh in January and February. They were both firmly of the opinion that keeping a sharp mind was essential for positive overall health and enjoyed teasing each other with small puzzles, humorous or devious, and oftentimes both. It was one of their own little personal 'things'.

Mac was preparing to close the shop for the day, going through locking up rituals long-ingrained within himself as Mari' finished attending to the necessary paperwork in the back office. He was ready to turn off the lights and exit with

Mari' through the back door when his mind turned, not for the first time this day, to the item he had purchased just that morning. Despite it being wrapped around carefully in soft cloth and placed securely in a padded carrier for him to take home to allow himself and Mari' the weekend and the space to study it in close detail, Mac could very easily recall the beautiful wooden box; painfully exquisite in its construction and detailing. There was no doubt whatsoever that it was an artefact crafted by a master carpenter.

The person who wandered into the shop with it was clearing an elderly relatives former home, having inherited it following his recent death. Recognising the box as a quality item, he was actually just looking for an initial appraisal to help decide him what to do with it. Mac was a very fair man and the foundation of their business success was in no small part due to its reputation for basic fairness. He gave the box a cursory inspection as he already knew that he greatly desired to own it. When he informed the young man who had brought it in to the shop that he would pay him 20,000 pounds for it, the deal was swiftly concluded. Mac was well aware that it may appear he had overpaid for it and that Mari' would have a loud opinion when she discovered the receipt of sale but he had concluded that there was an aspect of the item that was undeniably strange, and in his own very professional opinion, combined with his incredible knowledge, completely unexplainable. What was in no doubt whatsoever was the utter skill involved in its construction and the alluring beauty of it.

Every single moving part, and there seemed to be many of them just in the opening mechanism itself, was wooden. Tiny rivets, minuscule dovetails and a central dial with opposing corkscrew-type latches indicating open and closed had been lovingly created. There were some parts visible that were made from woods that Mac couldn't even identify and it was one of his fields of expertise. One thing was certain. If Mac had dated the item correctly, and of that he was sure beyond any doubt, then the artifact in the shop should simply not be there. It shouldn't exist.

Once they had returned to their home, a modest but spacious house which they had lived in since being married around 20 years previously, they both went about their own routines for an hour or so. Before cooking dinner together, a small habit of theirs that they indulged on the increasingly rare occasions when they were actually alone. They had found that it was another thing they loved doing together. When all was done and cleared, Mari' went upstairs to shower and prepare for bed, hinting seductively for Mac not to linger downstairs for too long, leaving little doubt of her intentions for him when he joined her in their bedroom.

Mac was sat at ease in the large and bright kitchen, sipping good strong coffee and considering the box he had purchased. Despite them both having agreed to look at it the following morning, as it was a Saturday, Mac felt like a child wishing he was able to open an Xmas present the evening before. There was a peculiarity about the item that was separate from its beauty, a thing that was not readily obvious.

It seemed to capture something more than the full attention of the person or persons admiring the craftsmanship involved and it had Mac hooked. He actually felt as though he was being gently pulled.

He was fast becoming convinced he could smell fresh wood-dust and a faint trace of pungent pipe smoke. He was sure that he could discern the sound of small flutes in the distance, amid other noises his mind identified as being that of a busy desert trading post. The snorting complaints of hard-worked camels, he could make out confirmed his conclusions, and he became aware that a fine sand floated in the air causing him to absentmindedly imitate the tightening of fabric over his face. He felt comfortable and looking down could see he was sat on soft, rich blankets. Mac was watching captivated as someone of high-skill cut a series of small, identical wooden squares. They reminded Mac of a chessboard except for the colours which resembled a pale silvery moon and a grey-hued mist rather than black and white. Mac was thinking that the new colours would look good on a board as long as the pieces matched the quality of the squares being formed when he was suddenly jolted back to reality by Mari', whose concerned voice had to be shouted into his face, followed by a stinging slap.

After several moments of confusion, Mac shook his head to clear out the last remnants of his daydream. He was astonished when Mari' told him that five hours had passed since she had retired upstairs. She had only came down to see if Mac had fallen asleep on the couch and had found him in a state she likened to hypnosis. They both agreed it was probably due to tiredness before looking at each other and then at the box. They had always been open and honest with one another and Mac voiced the conclusion they had both came to; there was some sort of enchantment surrounding this box and they were ill-equipped to handle such an Icon.

They agreed that first thing in the morning they would speak to a friend of theirs still lecturing at Heriot Watt, who would hopefully know what it was they were dealing with. He would certainly know more than they did but that was obvious due to the fact that they apparently knew nothing at all about it. As Mac lifted the deceptively heavy box over to the table, his hands lost their grip on it. Both he and Mari' watched in horror as such a beautiful thing fell onto the hard tiled floor with a crash which was solid enough that they both felt the vibration of on the soles of their feet. Amazingly, the only damage to anything was a little chip on the floor tile, whilst the box itself bore no marks at all and appeared the exact same. Another glance at one another spoke volumes. Placing it on the kitchen table, Mac gently covered it with the soft cloth again. He positioned the spotlight above the covered box in case they needed it in the morning.

That evening, Mac had a vivid dream in which he was actually a Sinbad-type merchant traveller in a magical land of flying carpets, lamp-encased genies, dreamcatcher-flutes and dragons. He was more than a wee bit disappointed when he awoke to normal life.

(FlatWorld),

There was much tension in the air, felt by both kingdoms. The GreySide Realm and the LightSide Territories were rife with suspicion. It had been fairly long since all-out war had existed between them, although there was always some skirmishes in the borderlands. The talk in the taverns and pubs was that full war was overdue. Even during worshipping services, the bishops of the Church-Cross were unconvincing in their assertions that it was foolish for either kingdom to wish conflict when the two realms were so strong. The everyday folks looked to their respective King and Queen for assurance, placing great trust on the Royal House of their born land. Both the LightSide King and Queen, and their sworn enemy, the King of GreySide and his own Dark Queen knew this well, and all of them respected it greatly.

King Grey and his Queen were satisfied with the strength of their armies, both in numbers and in skill. Great stores there were also, of grain and wine, and of weaponry; swords were sharp, spears were long and shields were sturdy. It had been long since the GreySide Realm had been so strong. Its principal city, where the Royal Court was situated, was large and pleasing to the eye. Wide avenues and large boulevards were central trading hubs, full of stores, taverns and eating areas. The kingdom had recovered fully and stronger since it's crushing defeat in the previous full-war between the two opposing forces. Practically rebuilt from ashes, the Grey Lands were of solid infrastructure, inhabited by hardy peoples and now wielded real power once more; stronger likely than the lands of light.

And there-in lay the problem, the catch-22, the catalyst for everlasting battle and death and the immobility of the reasons for perpetual war. The utterly defeated realm always recovered more powerfully than the Victors. Eventually, after some generations had passed, rising up and inflicting total defeat in return. Back and forth this pointless pain and slaughter had ever continued, unstoppable, lest unconditional belief was given over to the lore of the permanent-peace, which until now had seemed unlikely in the extreme.

However, be it enchantment or just sheer chance, but at the exact moment when Mac had dropped the box on the kitchen floor, lo,! The skies of FlatWorld had sent forth a cacophony of noise, with deep rumbling accompanied by an ear-splitting crack. Every inhabitant of FlatWorld felt the noise shaking their very bones. In addition to the physically manifested feeling still echoing in their bodies, all the way deep down in the part of the soul regarded as the 'Sixth-Sense', everyone bar none on the FlatWorld, at the very least had a fleeting thought about the peaceful legend as they had witnessed the precise definition of a thunderstorm without rain. Many of the inhabitants were dropped to their knees in wonder and prayers.

Both Royal Houses ordered the immediate assembly of their Senior Generals and Church-Cross Bishops. The King of the LightSide also summoned from his Eastern and Western Borderlands his own personal guards; two Knighted Warriors, who rode astride flying white Steeds of magnificent presentation. Beautifully saddled, and armoured around the face with leather of the highest quality, the muscular definition of the horses was perfection. The Light King was noticeably more relaxed with his elite guard beside his self. He had recently begun to suspect, and now feared, a special mission to assassinate him, leaving enough time of leaderless confusion in which the Dark GreySide infantry divisions, comprised of Warrior-Men commanding vicious GoblOrcs, to whom death in battle was an high honour, to overrun the White Towers and claim swift victory for the Grey King and Queen. His spy network had been reporting troop build-ups and deployments which were vaguely suggestive of such a tactical move, amid many other possibilities, however, but King LightSide focused his thoughts more and more on his own personal safety.

It was vital for battle plans to be both pro-active and re-active, whilst simultaneously remaining fluid to sudden changes in the tides of any fighting. The King of the LightSide refused to take any chances in conflict against the Dark GreySide beasts, as he thought disparagingly of the fighting forces commanded by his Royal counterpart.

He did have the right attitude, and grudgingly given respect, toward the Grey King's Royal Court, which was proper and just and as it should be; the King LightSide had an obligation to protect his civilian subjects and the Dark King would also have such. Besides, he and his Senior Generals all knew there were Warriors and Strategists of high calibre amongst his dark counterparts' senior staffing. The only troop movements by the GreySiders at present had been one division of infantry to battle readiness but they had been deployed just outside the main castle walls.

It was clear that they were undoubtedly just a small response to the deployment of two divisions of infantry made by King LightSide, which reached out as far as the central Borderlands. At that point in the assembly of his Senior-Staff, however, the King was notified by one of his spy-riders that another Infantry Division was being prepared for possible deployment by the Grey King, likely that direct opposition to their own troops at the Borderlands would be the obvious move. It was completely unknown at this time if any other preparations or arrangements for deployments were underway in the Grey Kingdom but the Light King's Generals clamoured loudly and insisted that he insert an elite Legion of mounted Knights in support of his Infantry immediately in order to contain any attacks should they happen.

His observant Queen became aware that the King LightSide was of a nervous disposition and although he was concealing it bravely. He was close to being overcome and paralysed by fear, positioning himself on the verge of a disastrous spiral into noticeable panic, something that would indeed guarantee total defeat.

The White Queen had been in pain, watching her husband's slow mental breakdown for months now and had went to great lengths to conceal the fact from everyone, particularly the Senior Generals. She had to act hastily lest the King's courage broke whilst in the presence of his Senior-Staff, so feigning sudden illness, the Queen appealed to her Royal husband to escort her to her parlour for a rest before his returning to the LightSide Council.

(Edinburgh),

In the Mackenzie home, in the kitchen, nothing could be heard, not even the very distant traffic. The house was altogether silent and still, as if holding its breath, but with complete ease. Mac and Mari' were both firmly and deeply asleep in the upstairs master bedroom, breathing softly in tandem with one another. Then, for a few moments there came a soft sliding sound, imperceptible to the house it appeared, which remained impassive, as did the comfortably sleeping occupants, who were both unmoving. It was most unlikely either of them would be slumbering were they fully aware of the powerful Bewitchment and Sorcery that they had brought into their home.

In the kitchen, the delightfully exquisite box dominated and it was from there that the gentle and inoffensive sound had whispered out from. After a short delay there came more quiet movements from within the box as if something akin to a game had started between unseen opponents. The actuality was that indeed a game had started and that game presented as chess, in keeping with a Black Enchantment that the inside contents had been cursed with.

The white Pawns, the Royal ones had both been moved forward and the grey Pawns likewise, although the Queen's Pawn was moved only one square whereas all the others were moved two. The white knight lifted as if by invisible hand and for a moment hovered above its starting square. It then smoothly and without sound unhurriedly glided into a position offering support to the Pawns already moved. The soft sounds of further movements inside the box continued for a while as the pieces retreated themselves back into their starting squares. The gorgeous, baroque pieces then vanished, reappearing instantly in the allocated storage-slots, which were meticulously created to accommodate each of the pieces by size and sophisticated shape.

The various testing, as that was what it was, of the basic mechanics contained within was because the Magicians-Enchanted Spellbound box had become firmly decided that a chance to demonstrate its powerful Bewitchment may be presented and so reset itself in readiness. The almost imperceptible sliding noises as it done so were again the only audible sounds in the otherwise silent home.

It was a serenity that was in direct opposition to the fear, suffering and anxiety afflicting the peoples of an entire dimension and world, contained, trapped and condemned in an ancient Spell-Binders' Chess set.

(FlatWorld),

Aside from his worrying about assassination and imagining mass attack, the King LightSide was becoming more and more paranoid. Until this moment only his own loving Queen was aware of the fact but she was now becoming convinced the signs foretelling the long-told legend exacerbated the affliction. Noises in the skies were not uncommon, albeit the recent worldwide savage thunder was unprecedented. She, like everyone else thought of the legendary words, but personally would pay more attention should another sun appear in the sky, which would indeed be a sight to see! A small smile at the thought of just how dumbfounded and stupid she would feel should such an event come to happen before returning to serious consideration. She was aware of the tension regarding the inevitability of all-out war between the two kingdoms and how clearly her husband was continuing to deteriorate whilst struggling under the pressure of his office. She determined to stand firm in her love and support for him.

She undoubtedly had more faith in the white armies at this point than her husband, the King. Turning his present fear into something which was obvious and fearless was her priority, lest the Senior Generals detected his distraction.

(6,000+years ago, on a realm named the GreenWorld),

A strangely attired visitor presented himself at the GreenWorld Palace gates, stating that he was far travelled from a long-distant place and had words for the King himself. He would say nothing more to the palace guard except for his name, which was given as Addarra-Cabbaddra. Nobody on the GreenWorld had ever heard the least rumour of him before now, despite him being a person of unusual and outlandish visage. He appeared to be unarmed, an extremely unusual choice for a person who wandered the wild-lands but after a short time he was granted an audience in the Royal Court with the Majesty of GreenWorld, named King Greenleaf.

He was a traveller, it emerged, but not simply between village and hills towards castle and walls. Addarra-Cabbaddra travelled between dimensions to other worlds, particularly worlds of a disposition where legend and mystique still lay in many places. He was in fact come to GreenWorld to exploit that very thing, its mysteries, and to essentially 'feed' upon primitive awe, and adulation. He required the raw emotions for actual sustenance and nutrition and the continuation of his long-lived being. He lowered his head as he thought, *as it ever had been and so it would ever remain*. This accursed information stayed undisclosed at all times and on all worlds.

His life was tied up with enchantment and sorcery; his parents had been cursed by a Master-Wizard that their firstborn son would bear this burden as penalty for an owed debt which was unpaid and forever would. It was granted that his parents love would be sufficient until his 16th year of birth. After that time Addarra-Cabbaddra was compelled to leave his own world or fade until death claimed him. As it now was, and as it would now remain.

Hurting and lonely, Addarra-Cabbaddra travelled into the multiverse, dwelling in a variety of strange places, feeding on the sparse applause garnered by skills of juggling balls and of accurate archery. He was resigned to this way of living when he met the person who showed him just how much Sorcery-skill and witchcraft was contained within himself, and taught him for many long years, converting the curse into a gift and educating him how best to wield this power. He never forgot however, how often he was shunned or violently rejected and how he had to endure ridicule and derision just to stay living.

Much time had elapsed since Addarra-Cabbaddra had bid farewell to that Sorcerer, the only person in the Multiverse whom he had considered truly to be his friend, Aleebba-Ba'Ba, who had been a manipulator of magic like himself, only far more powerful and competent. Aleebba-Ba'Ba had departed into the void on the day he had declared Addarra-Cabbaddra was fully-taught and ready to not simply walk his own path but to choose whichever paths he desired to walk upon.

No longer did he need to fear new worlds, to be afraid that his appearance alone would cause alarm or even hostility of frightening proportions where crowds of stone-wielding natives often scared and primitive. They were still single-minded in their intentions to kill what they couldn't comprehend or didn't understand. He had once spoken to Aleebba-Ba'Ba of the times he was assailed due to the ignorance and confusion of the primitive societies he encountered. Paradoxically, he was shown it was the emotional state of such people that enabled him to quickly absorb enough energy to enter the Multiverse again, resting awhile before selecting another realm to enter from the infinite choices available.

(Edinburgh),

Sitting together, sipping coffee, Mac and Mari' were preparing to telephone a learned friend regarding the unusual and exquisitely crafted box when it occurred to them saying simply that they were 'in possession of a box' would be wholly inadequate. Deciding to open the outer lock only in order to at least see what was contained inside seemed logical, as clearly something reasonably heavy was stored there. Switching the powerful spotlight on, Mac placed his hand onto the slide lock then halted. Interpreting his hesitant manner as nervousness, Mari' smiled at him softly. Placing her own hand tenderly on his, together they gently slid the lock mechanism from the area indicated as Locked over to the Open symbol.

They watched fascinated as a small device alike to a Portcullis gate rose seamlessly smooth until it was fully open. Many obvious clicking noises from within the box suggested marvellous complexity and that the opening sequence was continuing still. Suddenly, with a light whooshing that was felt on skin rather than heard, the sides opened up like book to reveal a silvery-white and grey chessboard of stunning beauty. As Mac and Mari' gazed in wonder at the bewilderingly detailed and unusually coloured pieces, they slowly disappeared from the richly velveteen storage slots they had been resting in and materialised on the board in the traditional starting positions for a game.

(FlatWorld Entered),

On an instinctive impulse, Mac lifted the silvery-white King's Pawn and moved it two squares forward, an oft-used opening in games. Mari' knew her husband's response to such a common move, so out of a sense of mocking fun about how well she knows him, with her own hand, she lifts his and guides him to his own Grey Queens Pawn in order for him to move it one square only, Macs' favoured response to such an opening from his opponent.

Their respective feelings fast turned to astonishment and also a sense of controlled panic. Without any fatalistic adrenaline surges of real fear present in their minds, they watched fascinated as the pieces moved themselves, unhurriedly but correctly, and paying proper attention to the stratagems being employed by each side. Suddenly the room glowed and shone and then felt themselves being pulled through an ethereal trapdoor.

With the sort of internal upheaval more commonly associated with an elevator ascending swiftly upwards, or driving at optimum speed over a humped-back bridge, the pair literally observed themselves entering into the pieces of the grey royal couple. When they surveyed one another, they were both attired as a King and Queen with the finest armour vaguely visible beneath cloaks of the richest fabrics, dark grey and bearing the logo of the Black-Cross of the GreySide Realm.

And when they looked up, there were two suns visible in the sky—one of which remained unmoving. That was the kitchen spotlight shining its message upon the enchanted and very old chessboard sitting open atop Mac and Mari's table. The QuietLight spoken of in the Legend of a Permanent-Peace was now burning bright and beautiful and proud.

(GreenWorld),

Addarra-Cabbaddra was most displeased with the King Greenleaf but he retained a neutral expression and a calm manner. However, outright rage was simmering within his self at the obstinate attitude of the King. It was infuriating to Addarra-Cabbaddra, who desired to feed; needed to feed to continue his existence and travelling that this closed-minded dotard upon the throne had completely dismissed his suggestion, offered in friendship, that he travel freely between the many Districts and Townships on GreenWorld to entertain the people, in the Kings name of course.

Whether the King was suspicious of Addarra-Cabbaddra or not is debatable because other forces unknown there were upon GreenWorld but His Royal Highness was very firm and very clear in his assertions that it was not an offer, nor even any simple suggestion that this strange visitor presented but an outrageously inappropriate request. And that was for someone unknown in the GreenWorld to wander where he wished to do whatever he desired, and all in the name of the King! Under Royal protection was a more accurate interpretation of how the King Greenleaf felt on the matter.

Had such a request been presented to the King Greenleaf by a known subject, it would be met by the same negative answer but accompanied also by a stinging public rebuke of his work ethic. All districts of the GreenWorld tended to their own routines, with fairs, gala-days and winter-mass aplenty. This outlandish and arrogant fool must consider them to be savages. Addarra-Cabbaddra was bade farewell and by Royal Decree ordered to take his leave and depart GreenWorld for all time.

The rage concealed within Addarra-Cabbaddra was now shown. No need had he for hysterical shouting or to engage in pathetic insult exchanges. Little heed did he give to the fact that he carried no weapon, large or small, because he wielded a power greater even than a Legion of full-armed mail-clad knights. With a casual wave of his hand and the utterance of some few words, the King Greenleaf and rest of the royal court present for this unusual conference were all struck silent-dumb and immobilised, unable to move mouth or limb. They were there displayed in the perfect definition of Petrified.

Despite Addarra-Cabbaddra being of a relaxed disposition, he was in fact spending large quantities of energy relative to the time and strength of the particular spells being cast. This was a base rule within the multiverse; energy must be equal and in balance. Henceforth he applied his curses speedily, but also cruelly, before departing from the GreenWorld.

Addarra-Cabbaddra condemned the GreenWorld to the seemingly never-ending divisions and suffering borne of warcraft and decried loudly that it should be severed immediately into two opposing kingdoms. The fact the GreenWorld was comprised of multiple orderly regions decided AddarraCabbaddra to think about the symmetry of a Chessboard and his will in the matter came to be. All people became immediately conscious of his spell-craft and were succumbed to hateful feelings of their close neighbours and to love only in their own chosen allegiance. The large and distant GreyLand area was instantly declared the enemy, and he supplanted distrust, malice and hate in place of the joy and carefree happiness that had existed, and also he ruined many men and animals by morphing large factions of them into GoblOrcs and Waargs. And with a ferocity felt as physical pain by members of the royal court under his current influence, he stated forcibly that the GreenWorld be named FlatWorld from that moment on, effectively imposing endless civil war upon an entire world in exchange for a few minor hurts to his ego.

There were criteria, parametres, rules, call them whatever, but they were immutable laws of the multiverse and they demanded there must be an opposing force to counteract Addarra-Cabbaddras incantation and it must be attainable to the person or thing on which the curse lay. On flimsy papyrus, the very same scraps of parchment-paper that were afterwards long held safe by the Dark Church Cross Bishops, who in fairness or perhaps because it was early in the conflict did afterwards draw accurate copies for their counterparts. He emblazoned hieroglyphics in the form of a devious puzzle to decrypt with the way to reverse all of the curses being the answer. Some pieces of the papyrus were unfortunately lost or decayed in the long years following, increasing the difficulty of the cunning puzzle.

Unknown as yet, childishly and like a slap across the metaphorical face of FlatWorld and the people who called it their home as a parting blow from Addarra-Cabbaddra to the long lost GreenWorld, should the time ever come that the puzzle was unwoven. He had not just worded the answer ambiguously, made deliberately vague and more difficult simply because it pleased Addarra-Cabbaddra to inflict such cruelty upon an entire world but he had further inserted a demand for a life of royal blood to be forfeited before restoration of the true kingdom can come to pass.

In the very moment he had made the preparations necessary for departing the now FlatWorld for all time, Addarra-Cabbaddra experienced a very strong future-vision he little understood, and so prepared to dismiss it from thought when suddenly, from out of the blue multiverse he found it further amused his cruel mind to plant the seed of a false legend in the ears of those present. Addarra-Cabbaddra had foreseen another star suddenly appearing in the sky of FlatWorld in his vision, so he insinuated that this heralded the return of the ever-peaceful GreenWorld. His anger would have been enormous had he been aware of the veracity of that particular statement.

(Edinburgh),

Mac and Mari' weren't actually absent from the kitchen as such, it was just that they were both absent from the dimension that the kitchen occupied in space. That however was a phenomenon for studying another time in another where and possibly even another 'verse. Anyone who entered the kitchen in the Edinburgh Dimension would obviously notice the chessboard but see nothing amiss. They would however feel an irresistible urge to leave it be, as well as a desire to exit that area; an instinctive reaction perhaps from the deepest part of the primal Being which detects possible danger.

The alpha-species from the Dimension Edinburgh existed in still had many evolutionary hurdles to overcome before attaining the ability just to accept the concept of the multiverse. And few more evolutionary steps would be required to attain the ability to fully understand exactly what the multiverse was, or crucially, what precisely it was not.

The ability to see and access its infinite wonders comes to pass for very few; sometimes from a mutational accident of birth like Aleebba-Ba'Ba, less often it was someone cursed, like AddarraCabbaddra.

For the most part, however, the multiverse was traversed, patrolled and even policed by exceptional people of countless worlds. Some were beings like Mac and Mari' and some others were of energy only, having evolved beyond the restraints or requirements of physical bodies. Some lifeforms of vast intelligence defied description but all of whom helped ensure balance was retained and every one thing reflected harmony regardless of the paths that the deeds of the Multiverse walked on.

(FlatWorld),

The appearance of the QuietLight had an effect unlike anything on the FlatWorld since the long ages-ago appearance and sorcery of Addarra-Cabbaddra. It stirred long-held disbelieving attitudes into dust, replacing them with wonder and, crucially, a high degree of expectation regarding the stability of life and prosperity, as is spoken of in the legend of the permanent peace. The masses knew nothing and cared even less about riddles imposed by some ancient conjuror of puzzles. And in any case would now reject any suggestion of it, accusing the royal houses of desiring only to retain power for themselves.

Ironically, the sudden presence of the QuietLight could draw the entire FlatWorld towards a war more fanatical and savage than any other conflict in its history, and one that it may never recover from, condemning the entire FlatWorld to a simple and primitive future, devoid of laughter and joy. It was essential that the royal houses make full use of the short time given to them before the population started to ask the questions to which satisfactory answers did not exist.

After the long hours of a whole day spent alone discussing then accepting their situation and then a further full day conferring with Senior Generals questioning Church-Cross Bishops and Senior Knights of the realm, Mac and Mari', now the GreySide King and Queen, were satisfied that from all the sparse snippets of papyrus and of information and rumour available regarding the unusually destructive manner of FlatWorld, the pair of them had concluded practically the same thing. Them being highly skilled at, if not obsessed with puzzles and games such as chess, they were both firmly of the belief that they and the LightSide King and Queen must have a personal meeting, as soon as could be, with both of them bringing their own Realm's Church-Cross Books for an united comparison by all four Royals.

King Grey King and his Queen thought that they had the ability to break the code if they could ask some questions of their LightSide Royal counterparts, and with luck, if not outright persuasion, the Grey King and Queen be granted access to look at the LightSide Church-Cross books in order to fill in the blank, damaged or just outright missing pages of the GreySide records. When the royal couple enquired about how communication with King LightSide and his Queen was instigated and how to arrange an official face-to-face conference, they were both happy with the answers.

They were also most intrigued by the venue such rare gatherings were conducted in: StoneHouse. They both dearly wished to hear and learn further of the lore connected with it as they listened intently to the Church-Cross Bishops limited description of the unattended and lonely house for royal use only and situated conveniently in the geographical centre of FlatWorld, reachable only by AirSteed flight.

Attending to first priorities, the GreySide Royals made the necessary bureaucratic arrangements for the request to speak with the King LightSide and his Queen. Considering the rarity of the event, the meeting of Royal Majesties was thankfully straightforward to arrange. An invitation would be dispatched. One the finest knights riding an AirSteed of proven and mighty stamina would be awarded the task.

Tradition stated the request be given over by words alone. The messenger knight remained until the answer, yea or nae, was spoken, and then he flew with the wind to deliver the response to his own King.

If the answer is Yea then the talks were expected by StoneHouse to be scheduled for the next morning. This was thought to be due to the fact that any plea for speech inside StoneHouse itself would be of great importance and as such deemed urgent but no-one knew for certain as it was a rare happening indeed.

On this occasion, on the return trip home to the Grey Kingdom, when seen from the ground and the rider was higher than the sparse clouds, the QuietLight reflecting on the polished armour of the knight relayed the impression of an unheralded and unusual shining-black comet streaking above the realm. The superstitious natives wondered what this particular heavenly-high display foretold and prayed for permanent peace with all their hearts, but the very same hearts were for a sudden moment gripped tightly by the unwanted but certain fear of treachery.

(StoneHouse),

The solidly erected StoneHouse was built immediately after the appearance of Addarra-Cabbaddra, possibly as a result of his cruel visitation or even in response to such, but that was unknown. What was known was that the laws of the house were said to be immutable and should be obeyed at all times. Only that was known for certain concerning StoneHouse, other than that it was for urgent royal use and even this was known only by the Senior Royal Court staff.

Its conception, its planning and its inordinately notable construction due to the logistically-challenging remote location were long forgotten, as was the visionary architect responsible for its design. This was the case because StoneHouse had many enchantments laid upon its own self, bestowing an aura of grace and charisma all around its locality. It represented and served no master, no kingdom nor royalty but the entire FlatWorld. The realm as a whole was its singular concern and StoneHouse was grieved deeply for the sorrow and despair it had ever perceived in the roots of the World.

The only price it asked in return, demanded in fact, was to observe and obey but above all respect StoneHouse rules. They were few in number and had been long-discussed by unnamed scribes of law preparatory to being decreed as rules, which were thenceforth literally 'written in stone'. These were carved into a large, in fact huge solid stone block which reflected delightfully in an harmonious silvery black colour, shimmering elegantly and with delicate hue; the Quiet Light has added an attractive artistic bloom of sorts, making it appear quite magnificent.

It was solidly positioned on a massive plinth directly outside of the entrance, where the one and only door in or out of the house was situated. Carved deep on the unusually coloured stone was declared boldly.

The use of StoneHouse by anyone out with royal bloodlines was not permitted. No combat nor weaponry of any sort was permitted inside StoneHouse. No falsehoods were permitted to be spoken within StoneHouse walls. Any oaths given within StoneHouse must be honoured.

Clear-written and impossible to misinterpret, the rules had the effect of ensuring a satisfactory level of trust was already engendered when both Kings and Queens entered the house and the heavy door was closed securely behind them. In the centre of the spartan yet somehow charming room was set four chairs, intricately carved and very comfortable. The four were arranged at a strong, spacious round wooden table of identical decorative style as the seating, and which offered adequate spacing for the High persons currently adjusting themselves into the richly padded armchairs.

Both couples felt at ease placing their respective archival books on the table, although both volumes remained closed and securely locked, at least until the necessary pleasantries and formalities had been attended to and then full attention could be turned towards the problematic reasons dictating why they were all four gathered in StoneHouse. The building gave the four a clear impression that StoneHouse had been fully expecting such a visit and had prepared the room accordingly.

Set slightly apart from the centre was another table, rectangular and longer than the central board, it was unadorned by any chair but had been laden with freshly prepared platters of cheese, meats, bread and honey. There were flagons also, of fine wine and fresh water, alongside an array of utensils, towels, wooden plates and goblets.

The scene, in such a calm environment, was extremely conducive for honest speech. The two opposing royal couples agreed that the long journey had given each an appetite and further assented that the breaking of bread and eating together was a perfect way in which to begin their assembly. There was a silent agreement between the four not to question how the food and other provisions were accomplished. It was probably because no answer would be given; the four royals each felt that in their hearts.

They each filled plate and goblet, enjoying the freshly-set offering from StoneHouse in friendship. By the time they were all four eaten and content, sat at the centre table with the remaining drinks in their sturdy goblets, the royals turned their conversation towards the reasons responsible for them being gathered, ironically, in such camaraderie; war, conflict, suffering, destruction, death and the possibility of the four of them possessing the means of bringing it all to a permanent and peaceful end, the time for which was limited.

(FlatWorld),

The previous day: The King LightSide was alone with his Queen in their private quarters. The Queen was absentmindedly musing over the perplexing issues affecting her beloved husband and King, and how best to focus his mind away from his ever-worsening conviction that assassination-teams had integrated themselves within his kingdom, ever seeking an opportunity to strike directly into the heart of their enemy. It was at this indecisive moment in the White Tower that a castle messenger arrived and informed the royal couple a sky rider knight was arrived from GreySide, bearing the Seal of the Dark King himself.

The Dark Knight begged urgent audience with the King and Queen, which was expedited at once. The haste was unnecessary to state, as the very presence of a Dark Knight inside of the White Tower Walls suggested it. Quickly seen and Swiftly answered, the Sky Rider departed speedily to relay to King Grey and his Queen that the news he bore from the LightSide Royal House was glad. They too also desired seeking the path to Permanent-Peace and would attend at StoneHouse, bringing the requested Book with them.

The King and Queen both agreed it was a real blessing from God that this opportune turn of events had occurred in the moment of their greatest need and the need of LightSide. The Queen, far less anxious than previously, understandably assumed the King would recover his full purpose now that there was a major event to consider and in this assumption she was correct. That evening she offered prayers to her God in humble thanks, for the restoration of her King, and in hope he may lead FlatWorld into a golden age of peace and prosperity, where happiness would live in the hearts of the people in places only hate had resided before.

Had the White Queen known fully the depth of her King's mind regarding the unusual situation facing LightSide, particularly the paths by which he had resolved to walk in order to forever put down the issues, then her mood would have been filled with a terrible but nameless dread. Despair she would have felt also but darkened by a bleakness lurking just out of her sight and grasp.

As for the White King, he felt a vigour burning in his heart like adolescent fire he had considered long extinguished and his step, like his mood, had considerably lightened. His dreams had been dark of late, and heavy indeed had been his burdens. Now he was certain beyond any doubt he had been carrying such cares as punishment for his being so blind to the solution for permanent-peace, whilst realising his dreams had actively tried to tell him of this. After the departed Grey Knight was long-flown away, curse his foul presence and odour in the fresh clear air of LightSide, the King felt elated.

The compromising mist that had covered his eyes and so badly blunted his perception had completely dissipated. He felt his mind was sharper than his now-restored vision, converting his elation into a kind of euphoria. He at least had no doubt of the path laid before him and intended to travel its full length until, one way or another, all was concluded regarding the unusual crisis faced by his realm.

He held an incredibly important meeting with his Senior-Staff before preparing for departure to StoneHouse. The King LightSide had given his final orders but wanted once more to firmly and sternly explain that they were vital, despite the murderous way that the objectives were to be achieved. His final words however were of encouragement, and a reminder that victory bestowed much glory upon Senior Generals and Church-Cross Bishops and Senior Knights too. The deeds of each after StoneHouse however were theirs to achieve, by whatever means each chose, as long as nothing remained.

Solid stone houses, whose construction would have been exceptionally arduous, time-consuming and a major cost to the Royal Purses, said to be under several forms of Enchantments, Come-Hither Enthralments and fascinating

Bewitchment, then being quietly set aside for short, once in millennia gatherings of royalty, were more than just a tad fanciful in his now logical, straight-thinking assessment, and treachery was what he feared betrayal by the Dark King. Well, the King LightSide was no fool and wouldn't be captivated by the alluring pull of beautifications surrounding a simple building. He considered the foundation of its personal bewitchment and enchantment to have been deliberately spoken words, mutated into legend by the slow turns of time.

In both kingdoms of FlatWorld, the Royal Air Steeds were groomed and adorned with the respective colours of their realms. In the quietest part of the day before dawn, despite the Quiet Light dispelling any sort of sunrise, two pairs of Royal Steeds leapt effortlessly into the morning air, offering minimal discomfort to their riders. The royal riders felt like a part of the graceful animals, with each of them feeling the raw power concealed within their SkyHorses, and so it was with comfort and confidence, each started out on the journey to StoneHouse; no-one in either pair had ever seen the dwelling to whence they were travelled to, adding to the mystique surrounding the journeys.

The huge amount of lore, which remained unknown regarding StoneHouse however, specifically the lack of compelling evidence or even whispered rumour of any sort of Charmed event occurring in the name of StoneHouse, had the effect of diminishing its perceived all-powerful magical powers in one of the visitor's minds. The King LightSide found it engrossing, yes, and fascinating too. But mesmerising, transfixing or even hypnotising, he was not willing to accept and utterly rejected the suggestion.

Thank the light heavens, he now knows the path unto Permanent-Peace. And even though so much blood must be spilled to obtain an end to war forever afterwards, including a significant amount of his own personal subjects, this high price must be paid, and then must be tolerated. And he vowed to himself that he would pay the price demanded in blood and misery in order to bring about lasting peace. It would be the burden of others to give their life's blood and to tolerate the pain involved. His own duty simply lay in deciding and then giving the orders to march out his armies.

As was mentioned, before departing from the White Tower, the King LightSide had conference with his senior generals and strategists. He had informed his Queen it was regarding day-to-day operations and bade her leave the chamber to oversee final arrangements for the journey to StoneHouse. The White King then for the final time, to minimise confusion and misunderstanding, went through the relatively straightforward invasion plans he had drawn up against the Grey City and the foul Dark Forces' Castle, the Royal Tower and its government houses.

Then by extension the entire kingdom would be fallen, and then, this time, the King LightSide would ensure its fall would be so low it could never again rise. He had finalised the details only several hours previously. They needed to be easy to understand, and just as easy to implement.

The shortness of time had the unexpected advantage of the invasion being a complete surprise, which increases the effectiveness of the attack. The Grey Kingdom would also be bereft of any effective leadership for the first crucial strikes against it. The White King smiled at the thought, congratulating himself for being so visionary and decisive.

How loved he would be, with all people singing songs of his deeds, and giving him great praise.

The GreySide King and his Queen would be at StoneHouse, totally unaware that as they were sitting playing games with ancient scraps of parchment-paper their realm had been all but ended and they were both his prisoners to be taken to the White Tower. Firstly though, they would be paraded through the central thoroughfare for the people to see for themselves the totality of his victory.

The King LightSide was pleased with the thought of such an achievement, and was noticeably more excitable to his Queen as they prepared to leave for the meeting with the GreySide Royals. For no other reason of obvious means she felt a thrill of disquiet run from her stomach into her heart, causing her to experience an awful moment of disorientation during which she seen her husband sitting proudly, but on the Black Throne, with his face twisted in rage and with hate in his previously shining eyes.

(StoneHouse)

Having broken bread together, and raised goblets in toast to friendship for all time, the four royals were well-met and spoke of the reasons that had conspired to bring them into this union. Much was said but much more was unsaid as a sudden feeling of urgency was felt by both the GreySide Royals.

King Grey proposed that his Queen peruse the book brought by the white royals, who in turn were welcome to scrutinise the GreySide Records. The King Grey and his Queen exchanged a strange look as the White King declined to study the Grey Book but bade them welcome to survey the white. The King LightSide cited illiteracy as his reason for having no desire to look at Books of papyrus, and declared his White Queen was the same, but they both agreed and assented to the Grey Queen comparing the pages. Eagerly, but oh so carefully the Queen immediately begun to conduct the process in the brisk methodical way Mari' would approach such a task. In the end, the other three simply left her to the workings.

The King Grey because he knows his wife and Queen and there was no-one more accomplished than she to attend to the puzzling scraps of fragile parchment-paper.

The King LightSide appeared distracted and detached from this undoubtedly vital important process, as if disinterested, something that evidently confused his Queen, although she was attempting desperately to conceal the fact. The King Grey clearly sensed her conflicted state however and couldn't prevent the sudden and unexpected thought entering into his thinking that something was badly wrong.

Now that he was become aware of some inconsistencies, he fought hard to prevent himself choking. Treachery from a person of Pure-blooded lineage would be disastrous; Treachery from a King would be fatal.

King Grey now recollected the Queen LightSide making reference to the Books of the Church-Cross when first they were arrived and all had entered StoneHouse, placing their respective archival Books on the round table. She had known that the pages were relatively few, but there were contained therein many letterings of cunning writing. She offered also an accurate concluded opinion on which particular section was lost, and spoke briefly of studying the book in previous years.

The King Grey realised this was not illiteracy in any sense of the word. This then meant the White King had broken not only the relatively minor but nonetheless compulsory and expected rules of Royal etiquette which dictated their behaviour, but also a base Law of StoneHouse regarding Falsehoods, by stating firmly, before his Queen spoke in contradiction to his clear-spoken insistence that they both were unable to read or write!.

King Grey was reeling in anger, but there was fear there too and it remained the strongest emotion; if the White King had Lied within StoneHouse walls, then he was arrived there with Treachery already decided in his heart. Who would know what other Laws he was willing to ignore and break. Or possibly even had already broken! It was essential the Dark King keep these suspicions from his Love, his wife.

The Grey King prayed silently that his Queen, Mari', would unravel enough information in order to proceed with their attempted restoration of true peace on FlatWorld. Not just an uneasy truce betwixt kingdoms that continued to harbour distrust in one another, and that fostered ever-worsening anxiety within the hearts of the peoples, but a True-United World of bright happiness. He glanced at his beautiful Wife, and felt at that moment just how deep his own Love for her actually went. She offered him a small smile of encouragement. He was heartened in a way that brought tears to his eyes, and knew he would freely-willing offer up his own life if it saved hers. Such Regal beauty should be preserved, and admired. She, indeed, was a Queen that would be loved by all, whether from the Light or the Grey.

(Edinburgh),

The Chessboard still remained on the spot atop of the Mackenzie's kitchen table. The intricately carved pieces had been undergoing a series of moves, despite anyone even being present to witness the movements. Many of the Grey pieces were either remained on their own starting square, or positioned where they had little or no relevance. The Grey King and Queen seemed slightly isolated and unprotected, leaving the King vulnerable to sudden attack. The positions being assumed by the White pieces indicated that quick and sustained assaults on the Grey King piece itself, and the hugely depleted GreySide back-line, would likely result in the desired victory if the attack was very swift and very brutal, and, most importantly, unexpected by the Grey King and his Queen.

The LightSide pieces on the Chessboard did of course attack both the Dark King and his Queen, and sought to gain complete control of the GreySide territories. The assault was swift and unexpected, and it successfully achieved its objectives of having the Dark GreySide Royals separated off the White forces inhabiting the squares surrounding the sad and lonely looking pitiful Grey pieces left.

The board continued to be lit by the strong spotlight above which was focused on the scene. It was now far too hot to handle with uncovered skin, and the small fuse hidden in the three-pronged input plug which connected to the electricity supply was struggling to control the amount of current running through its delicate wiring, with the 'trip-switch' primed to shut it all down, including the light itself. For the present however, all was of calm manner in the Mackenzie household.

(FlatWorld),

The assault on the GreySide Realm was already begun, with unstoppable and seemingly endless Legions of Infantry and Divisions of fanatical Religious War Men, all being protected and supported by twin Battalions of Elite Knights dominating the airspace above the fighting. The unprepared and practically undefended Grey Towers were close to being taken, with the rest of the Grey City having been completely demolished, and burning into ashes.

The routes through the GreyLands by which the various enemy forces had taken on their way to the Grey-Towered Capitol City were evident by the sheer depths of destruction inflicted, as was the off directions journeyed to the other larger Townships. Cities, market-estates, villages, rich mansions, farms and ranches, it mattered not; everything with even the remotest possible use was razed flat into useless rubble and broken wood. On the White Kings orders all was then burned into nothing but heat-broken stones, dust, and ashes.

Sadly, the King LightSide had also ordered a series of unfortunately horrible events involving mass genocide. He considered the Dark forces inhabiting the GreyLands as subhuman savages, save for a very few Senior Staff and Royals, so had subsequently ordered the immediate annihilation of every inhabitant, bar none, of the GreyLands. Men, Women, Children, including babies still clinging to their Mothers bosom were killed. Many Women were brutalised in unspeakable manner beforehand. Even the animals were slaughtered and burned, including any pets wandering around aimlessly, vainly attempting to find their Masters, whom they likely ended up being burned alongside with, or buried beside in massive Graves, deliberately unmarked.

King LightSide was fully convinced that the absolute extermination of the Enemy, including the complete destruction and levelling of their land, former buildings and achievements were the requirements needed to create the path leading to everlasting Peace. Surely! If there was no enemy to defend against, then the armed forces could be all stood-down and the day of victory be celebrated every year He had vowed to himself that he would not allow his steps to falter at the last, and those steps would be held firm by the strength of his conviction.

The White Tower walls would be adorned with flags and banners honouring his great victory upon his return. He would then assume the title of Absolute Ruler of the entire FlatWorld. Oh! How the peoples would shower him with praise. And yea, he would proudly accept their loud, clamoured worship and words bestowing much honour on him as he continued leading them unto everlasting Peace. Wallowing in personally given pride, and fantasising of his greatness, he further envisaged himself being known and considered by all to be a wise and benevolent Ruler, kind and fair to all but with an iron fist against wrongdoers.

He had never heard the word 'Hubris' on FlatWorld, but in his head was immersing himself deeply in its deceptively inviting charms, and full-enjoying anticipating the experience of having everyone's Praise bestowed upon his own self.

(StoneHouse),

Mari', the King Greys Queen was determinedly attempting to gain his attention without alerting the White King or Queen. She was both elated and frightened; elation was fine, but the King Grey had never seen fright afflicting his Queen, so he made his way towards her, under the pretence of refreshing her goblet of water. He looked at the table, and though he didn't understand what he was surveying, it was obvious from the way that she had arranged the papyrus scraps that there was contained there a message that she was able to interpret, but didn't want the White Royals alerted as yet, if at all. With strong suspicions of something wrong still fresh on his mind, the covert way in which his Queen brought him to her side had condensed those feelings into certainty that something of great importance was amiss, yet he knew not what it was.

Over many long years of happy and adventure-filled marriage, Mac and Mari' had obviously come to know each other inside and out, and knew well the meaning being conveyed by certain actions of theirs. Clearly the Queen wished for private talk, and when the Royal Greys glanced over to the LightSide couple to see if they were paying any sort of close attention, they were grateful to observe that they were firmly engaged in their own strangely whispered and furtive conversation. It was plain to see that the White Queen was significantly upset about something, but her King and husband would have to endure and manage her grievances, as it was evident that for whatever reasons, it was he she was upset with.

Using minimum wording, the King Grey listened intently as his Queen explained the complete set of papyrus revealed only one possible answer, but that too was a puzzle in the form of a Conundrum to decipher, and she had been unable to obtain a grasp of any sort of meaning from the words that Addarra-Cabbaddra had long ago concealed within the papyrus scraps. The initial solution spelt out the following sentence "Love must Die to give Life to Love". The King Grey squeezed the hand of his Queen to offer comfort and support to her, and assuring her he retained happy confidence in her thought processes 'breaking down the walls' of any challenge put in front of her. Unbeknownst to the Grey King, his Queen had in actual fact already totally dismantled the walls of the challenge, and had fully-opened the answers to Addarra-Cabbaddras' ages-old enigma, but faced real difficulty being anywhere near happy about it.

Crestfallen, she understood too well the last, bloody demand, and that it must be met in order to completely break the ancient Curse. A Bewitchment containing power enough to condemn an entire World for thousands of years, like FlatWorld itself had already endured, could not be broken by any counter-spell, or in any way, other than the path demanded by the Enchantment laid upon it.

She wished it was not so, but in her present advent as the Grey Queen, combined with being inside of StoneHouse, she was aware that if she looked deep inside her mind then she was able to discern the lives of previous Grey Queens and some cognitive thoughts from them, like a distant inside-echo of enlightenment. It had felt like innumerable past Royals were trying to help her, but it had only succeeded in awakening the pain of all past Queens in her own heart, and the untold depths of their torments was grievous to bear. The Grey Queen offered them into her heart, letting them know she too was enduring the same hurts.

The appalling pains felt by Mari'/the Grey Queen were sharp and acute, actually causing her to momentarily gasp for air. The thought of so many people dying so young for so long. The grief!, the sheer distress, it was lying over all the Lands during all this time, like an unseen but mighty burden blanketing the anguish of the brutally Cursed FlatWorld. Exacting its own toll on all, soldier or civilian, rich or poor, it limited all happiness, stunted desire for growth, and diluted the want for love and joy. It was like a fine mist diffusing the Sunlight and diminishing its effects on the whole World.

The sheer dignity of this incarnation of the Grey Queen brought forth from her a silent pledge, an asseveration to herself, that if she were the Queen of a realm then she would fulfil her Royal duties to serve the people. She too, like the White King, took an oath to herself not to let her step falter when the time came that the people needed her to stand firm, and that oath was taken within the walls of StoneHouse. She wanted to let the King Grey know everything now, but deemed it essential for him to remain oblivious still. Tears of sorrow, and despondency came from her beautiful eyes. The Grey Queen had been considering the implications of the words contained on the papyrus scraps, and hoped only for her King, her beloved husband, to go forward with pride when all was over and done.

Apart from the answer to the ancient puzzle, the papyrus scraps had much to tell whomever unravelled its secrets. She was aware for instance that the White King had lied and spoken untruths at table, although she knew not what form or

50

shape punishment from the Enchantment of StoneHouse would manifest as. She was further aware that the White Tower had ordered every Army-Group to battle, with the terrible orders to kill and burn everything that they encountered. She knew that by this time they had likely succeeded in conquering the entire GreySide territories, including the Royal Houses and Castle. Looking over at the White King and Queen, it was very clear that the Queen knew nothing of any events occurred whilst they were met with their Royal Peers at StoneHouse and was being appraised of them at that time, as her anger at her husband and King was palpable.

Despite the LightSide King assuring her that the hated Dark GreySide Royals were completely unaware of their own Doom, her embarrassment at his actions caused her to practically choke with humiliation when the Grey Queen offered her more water, and although it was in order to assess her attitude to the News her King had spoken, the kindness was real. The awkwardness and agitated manner of the White Queen, her discomfort, and her shame too, brought a warm and essentially understanding smile from the Grey Queen as she refreshed her goblet, recognising her ignorance of any Warcraft so henceforth her complete inability to effect change to any of her Kings Battle-orders. Far more Importantly to the GreySide Queen, Mari', was that the White Queen was more concerned about her husband's disdain for the rules of StoneHouse than she was about his Betrayal of the Grey King and Queen, of which her shame was real also.

This was vital for the execution of the plan Mari' had conceived of, based on her own translation of the long-hidden Conundrum which had been revealed at last. 'Love must Die to give Life to Love'; she had found it incredibly easy to decipher and understand. Her husband, the King Grey, had much to occupy his attention as the prime royal, so consequently had forgotten that it was an Enchanted Chessboard box that was responsible for their being where and what they were. Fortunately his Queen was a woman of wonderful substance and wit and she was able to keep part of her mind in their own world. For how much longer she did not know, so was happy with the acceleration of the goings-on and happenings.

It was becoming extremely apparent to the Queen, Mari', that the longer they were both on FlatWorld the more difficult it was to remember their previous lives. Mac was dangerously close to being taken over completely as the Grey King and she herself was using all the strength she had to remain focused on her plan. She instinctively knew it was the correct solution and StoneHouse had a part to play but what shape it would take she knew not. She did know that the moves would occur soon, and when they did, everything would happen quickly, as each person present acted and re-acted to the situations as they evolved.

(Edinburgh),

In the Mackenzie home, each room was unchanged and nothing was moving. Except in the house kitchen and the chessboard atop of the large table, where the majority of the pieces were returned to the storage slots they were in before appearing on the board in the regimented starting squares assigned to each. There were many more grey pieces in storage slots than white. On the board itself a match had reached the point of a fierce endgame with the Grey King piece under pressure of Check-Mate but presently being valiantly protected by the Grey Queen. Only one isolated Grey Knight remained but it was unable to move without his capture and Death.

The game continued in the kitchen, with the LightSide King utilising both of his knights in his final assault to claim Check-Mate and total victory, and cleansing his territories of all the despised GreySide beasts. Anyone who knows chess would instantly see that White was poised to win in three moves or less, with the Knights now in position offering a clear path for the White Queen to slide beside her husband, the King LightSide, to Check and offer no move to the King Grey except sacrifice and his own inevitable death. As this was happening, the spotlight above was so hot that small tendrils of smoke slid from the bulb, and the plug socket had begun to spark slightly. Events occurring on FlatWorld seemed far away.

(FlatWorld),

The slaughter had been terrible. Vicious GoblOrcs and Waarg-Masters had been wholly unprepared for the sudden and unexpected attacks and were succumbed in short order, Divisions of Infantry were overrun with minimal fuss, and the GreySide realm forces were entirely overwhelmed and utterly defeated in less than a single day. The horrors of the genocide of unconditionally surrendered soldiers was thoroughly grotesque, with the condemned GreySiders, including the Church-Cross Bishops and Senior Generals being summarily executed whilst lost in the confusion at such repulsive and murderous actions, all of which were borne of betrayal by High-Royalty.

The rank smoke which came from the burnings left the scent of death and dying across the entire realm. Verily all was now of a truly grey colour as the enormous plumes of ash settled on everything. Where it was fallen, breathing life was ended as it choked river, stream and road, suffocating the already desperately grim land. It was a scene from hell and nothing moved within it.

(StoneHouse),

It was started by the White Queen ironically, who, puzzled and innocently asked aloud of everyone if there was a hint of smoke-smell in the house, as no fireplace was built there in StoneHouse that they could see. The White King, her husband, was readying himself to quickly answer in the negative when the GreySide Queen abruptly, verging on rudeness, and most certainly against all royal court etiquette bade him to remain silent, unless his wish was to speak further fabrications within StoneHouse. The King Grey was initially horrified by such a flagrant breech of Court behaviour by his Queen, but then had a moment of clarity, realising it was Mari' whom had interrupted and therefore something of great importance had, or was occurring.

He connected her action to the disquiet he had been feeling but still couldn't find anything seriously amiss in which he was able to coalesce his fears around until he realised, like Mari' had before him, that FlatWorld was taking them bit by bit, integrating them into the person they are in this dimension. He tried to think of his actual life in Edinburgh and found that he could barely recall anything else other than that he was named Mac. He was only left with the hope that his Queen had retained a grasp of their own lives, as his momentary clear memory was now faded. He was King Grey and was thinking with pragmatism of his and his Queens position, as far as he was able to.

When he considered his Queens assertions regarding the King LightSide speaking aloud untruths since they had all four of them full-entered StoneHouse, he experienced the most nauseating disorientation of his life, and was noticeably shocked as he instantly perceived all the implications of the White King lying, and combined with the now undeniable hint of smoke-smell in the house he knew he was indeed Betrayed, and the GreySide Realm was already lost.

It had taken time for the King LightSide to recover his wit following the Grey Queens unexpected interruption, and his shock at hearing her speak of being so aware of his mendacity. He was presently considering the ramifications of her knowing his spoken words had been intended to mislead, and was decided that it mattered not, as by this time his victory would be completed and his Greatness assured. In fact, the White King decided the time was come to inform the King Grey and his disrespectful Queen of the happenings befallen their now former realm. If the Dark Queen, curse her perceptions, had an opinion that displeased him then he would remove her tongue with his own blade.

He turned to see where the Royal Greys were stood. His intentions to parade the Dark Royals as prisoners before condemning them to a cold existence in a dark dungeon was now rejected due to his anger, because they represented the pinnacle of the former GreySide, and because he had no intention of displaying what would effectively be evidence of his Betrayal, something he intended to forget as soon as possible and of which his people would never know. There was no-one left in the Grey Kingdom to cause Martyrdom to be a concern, but he was resolved to now end the life of the Grey King. He slid from his boot a slim long-bladed dagger he had concealed there and made his way towards the GreySide Royals.

King Greys Queen had gripped his arm tightly and removed them both into the farthest corner, talking rapidly. She was having to concentrate on wording the predicament they faced as though primarily addressing the King Grey, as little hope she had left that in Mac's mind he was anyone or anything else. The King Grey was reeling still from the news that the White King had spoken untruths at the table and the sure inevitability of total defeat befallen them. What the King was unaware of was just how utterly defeated he was, and the unspeakable manner of how it was achieved. This was what his Queen was urgently trying to inform him of; the White King was insane, and had concluded that the utter removal of an entire people, of which he had achieved, would bring about the lasting peace, and thus bestow upon himself great honour and Praise.

Mac and Mari' had in their previous Lives been of high intelligence and this remained the case on FlatWorld. It required little time for them both to understand what the White King had planned and what his subsequent move must be, which would be an assault on the King Grey himself. Indeed, they could see him approach at that moment, smiling as if greeting an old and much-loved friend.

(FlatWorld),

It was around dawn, although the exact time of daybreak was now obscured for the birds and macho farmyard Roosters. Not only because of the QuietLight of legend, but the thin haze of smoke which blurred the entire horizon. Where lands ended and the sky started was impossible to tell through the orange tinted smoke which deceived the usual Avian choruses heralding the coming of the Sun. Sounds were damped everywhere, but there was little appetite for unnecessary talk in the White Army-Group ranks.

There was a feeling running through the LightSide peoples of uncertainty and disquiet. Rather than the expected victorious delight, comrades and confederates from the entire White Realm were acting as though waking-up from a collective, communal mass-dream, more dazed than anything else but with an urge to detach and disassociate themselves from any part played in the past days. Many awaited news from the White King, and there gathered a large crowd outside of the white towers. Strangely, most people unhurriedly returned to their own duties and responsibilities, attending to the daily routines with an almost monotonous languor.

(StoneHouse),

The King LightSide was nearing the GreySide Royals, his Queen was approaching too, but slightly behind the King, so she didn't really occupy anyone's mind. The scene that swiftly followed was complicated, but the White King suddenly leapt effortlessly towards the King Grey and felt his long blade pierce full-through his chest, except that when he looked at the King Greys eyes as he twisted his knife it was the GreySide Queen looking back at him, dying, but smiling. She reached out her hand and the GreySide King took it. He wept as she then passed from life.

Laying down her pale hand across her chest and crossing the other over it he stood up tall and faced the White King, whose weapon was remained in his Queens chest. It was apparent to the three Royals that the Grey Queen was fully aware of the intended treachery, but the White Queen was furious because she was not. The King Grey ignored her. His business was with the White King, who still looked amazed that his Betrayal, and more, was known to the Grey Queen, who had sacrificed herself by rapidly moving afront of her Kings position to knowingly give her life for the Man, and King, that she had loved.

(Edinburgh),

The house had now acquired an empty feel. The rooms remained silent. Except for the kitchen, from where several sounds crept out from. None were loud on their own, but put together resulted in a slightly clamorous noise. There was another flurry of activity on the Chessboard, although that had ceased suddenly. The sparking on and around the spotlight plug socket was intensified and sounded like lots of small twigs being snapped. It couldn't last much longer and it didn't!. A loud bang and a large amount of acrid smoke surrounded the socket. The overheated light shattered into tiny myriad pieces of glass which momentarily resembled glitter, and finally the light was extinguished. It took a short time for the smoke to clear totally, but when it did it revealed a curious sight.

The fine shards of glass had burst out all over the kitchen table, but there was a complete, exact circle around the Chessboard, as if it had been covered, or perhaps protected by a forcefield similar to the Earth-Dimensions magnetic fields which deflect radiation, visible as an Aurora at both poles. However its Enchantment shielded it, the Chessboard still remained exquisite, and would be capable still of drawing admiring looks even from non-chess players. On the Board itself only very few pieces were remained, with another curious sight to be seen.

The White King had made a terrible blunder and had all too eagerly played what he thought was the penultimate move before Checkmate. In his haste the King overlooked the most basic of last-minute Chess stratagem, and had taken the bait of the Grey Queen offering to sacrifice. He had thought to make his Superiority all the more crushing to his beaten opponent and all too late did he realise his error. His anger at losing the victory in the manner he had was fearsome. The King Grey was left with no move to make that escaped Checkmate, courtesy of the White King assuming his own personal Victory was there for him, he need but only reach out his hand and grasp it. And so the match was drawn via the route of StaleMate. It could be considered that a balanced peace was won for both sides.

(FlatWorld),

There was no warning for anyone to cover up their ears as the noise was unexpected. An explosive bang was heard and felt by everyone, followed by a sudden darkness falling. The ringing in people's heads persisted for hours, but wit had not deserted them and all perceived that the QuietLight had gone, disappeared as fast as it had first burst into life in the sky. People lit lamps and candles and wondered what this now meant for them.

Magical powers still existed, and what persons there were left on FlatWorld still awake alerted the sleeping. All persons came outside and watched fascinated as hundreds of thousands of shooting stars filled the Dark night in a glorious display of colour. The QuietLight had dispersed with hypnotic beauty, as though signalling the coming of better times, because the end had filled hearts with joy, and renewed hope for something else that was better.

The very many people that had lived through the experience returned to their own lands to await News. The Legions, and others who resided in the White City, wondered what the morning would bring about, and what would say the King LightSide about the situation that now existed within, and also without the kingdom. Returned forces were telling of the terrible slaughter, and all the speech of the events being spoken of raised only more questions, all pertaining to the King LightSides role in ordering such monstrosities, or even allowing them to occur in his Name. Surely!, thought they, the Grey King himself had manipulated a plan of dark and devious cunning, which must have somehow went awry and caused the gruesome deeds. All who gathered at the White

Tower Walls had to wait awhile longer than expected for the return of the King.

(StoneHouse),

The situation continued to evolve apace but it was in no way that any of the royals could have expected. Before any of them could make further movements, especially the King Grey, whose grief and anger was overwhelming at the loss of his beloved Queen. The time had arrived for StoneHouse to be involved, and it now started to fulfil its own purpose; a single purpose conceived of long-years since. Saddened would be the Shaman who bestowed upon every single stone, and all the other materials used to erect StoneHouse, the ability to break Addarra-Cabbaddras' wicked Curse that Millennia had passed, and only now was the Counter-spell being utilised, but gladdened also that at last, the end was approached.

A deliberate sound from the central round table alerted the three Royals to the beginning of something unlooked for, as a bright light of the deepest hue of green was there, and that seemed to hover softly just above the table top. The all three of them instinctively knew that this was the doing of StoneHouse and made their way over to the table in order to see more clearly what activity was there occurring. With previous grievances set aside, it was with genuine awe that they witnessed a phenomenon beyond the ken of any of them, as it was a display few would understand or even imagine.

The nearest approximation of what was in front of their eyes would be a Hologram of stunning capabilities, and it seemed to know who was present and what each of them was.

Spinning slowly, the first noticed stunning green colorations were like a thin mist which moved around in a now expanded and loosely circular shape, large enough for a full-grown man to stand inside its mesmerising shell. And lo! There was stood upright the image of a man, attired in a thick hooded robe which concealed his face. The only visible part of him was his large hands, held clasped as if in prayer.

The figure presented as a flickering, slightly opaque blue of many shades, and radiated a welcome feeling of comfort. Within that reassurance there was an undisputable power concealed, and it was felt by all three who were impressed by the sheer depths of capability they sensed from the created image on the table. It wasn't noticeable if his feet were in contact with the wood or slightly the surface, and his long robe added to the illusion of him hovering. Regardless of that small matter, what was in no doubt whatsoever was the Nobility present in the proud bearing of the effigy before their own eyes. They all three were suddenly startled when he spoke to them, bidding them to be seated and warning against any interruption unless invited to talk. He said these words to all three but looked only at one, the White King. He then told them his name, which was Hansel.

With each Royal seated, Hansel spoke. He told them first of his creation, enabled by the Sorcery-Skill imbued into StoneHouse, whose purpose was to break the Curses of Addarra-Cabbaddra. No doubts had they that it was truth being said when the Hansel-figure told them that, such was the love, understanding and respect that was borne for the very lands and waters which provided the bounty that the people of GreenWorld required, to live their own lives in plentiful comfort, that a consciousness of sorts developed in soil, rock and tree. It was a consciousness of growth, of renewal and protection, and it was suspected, correctly, by GreenWorld itself that the traveller Addarra-Cabbaddra was also a Necromancer of evil intentions. Short was the time GreenWorld had to make arrangements to preserve itself, but with the assistance of the unnamed Shaman, the instigation of constructing StoneHouse was managed, with the materials used in the engraving of the Rules all being especially blessed. It was the first time anyone had heard the Conjurors name uttered for 6,000 years, and the story of his visitation to GreenWorld was wholly unknown to any Royal.

Astonishment each Royal felt at hearing FlatWorld had once existed in harmonious splendour, where Grey and Light were mere shades of colour rather than kingdoms in conflict against each other.

Amazement after amazement they felt as they were given many details and historical lore of GreenWorld, a joy filled habitat of wonderful vitality, where there existed no weapon of War, nor indeed any word to describe Warfare of any sort. There lived no-one on the entire fertile GreenWorld who wished conflict against their neighbour's house. A world truly rare amongst countless number of others. Hansel spoke of the happiness of GreenWorld, and then the sadness the loss of such happiness brings. Soft was his tone when he spoke about the passing of such glad-hearted life.

The countenance of Hansel then became stern, and streaks of the darkest black appeared periodically within the green sphere around him, like a twisted Shrike's dancing across the surface, drowning in its own existence. Hansel opened his arms out wide, but it was a stance devoid of any welcome. The all three Royals felt not greetings in the gesture either but the coming of Judgement, bearing either earned goodwill or deserved wrath. The all three could feel the life StoneHouse possessed awakening its own tongue, ready to speak through the Hansel-Conduit it had created for that very purpose. Using the powers from the Enchantments laid upon each and every stone used to build it so long ago, when the Hansel figure next spoke, it was the word of StoneHouse which was heard, and paralyzing was the strength of voice that spoke. And yea!, Judgements became real, sentences were passed, and retribution was had. Punishment was harsh, but reward there was too.

(FlatWorld),

All could sense somehow, or feel, the culmination of great events was at hand. Great anxiety afflicted the lands, and it seemed like everyone and everything had drawn in a deep breath, and there came a brief moment when it felt as if the very World itself had stopped. Change there would be when the new day broke, but of what manifestation the FlatWorld knew not. Uncertainty at the unknown quality or shape of the approaching Doom filled every heart. Household pets were shrank into their Masters laps, and the beasts and birds outside were subdued, or hidden in Burrow or Barn. A time was come that would decide the future, and lay down the path to be walked, be it in bleakest dark or glorious light, for each person and every generation thereafter.

(Edinburgh),

Fortunately it was that someone would have to possess the ability to travel through the multiverse to observe the energetic happenings inside of the Mackenzie household, as from each window there blazed hypnotising streaks of special beauty. The origins were specifically from the kitchen, but such was the build-up of electrical-like vibrancy, ribbons of green and blue fizzled along falls and ceilings like live wires writhing from the sheer power surging through them, and pulsing out energetic colours the full length, coating the whole of the inner walls in potent brilliant Aurora, and formidable might was contained therein. Verily, there existed within that strength the ability to travel through the multiverse, but no-one was there in that Dimension with the compulsory knowledge, never mind the essential wit called for in order to perceive the Doorway that was there for the opening. Many people passed through the wonderful Glow but it remained invisible to all, although some may have been uplifted for reasons that they knew not, and would feel lighter of footstep thereafter. Periodically, someone's pet dog would be startled, or bark at nothing, but even the keen senses of animals detected nothing amiss.

(StoneHouse),

The Hansel-Conduit spoke, and none would dare interrupt, even if they could. The reasons given lent it every right there was, and each awaited for the fate allocated to themselves in silence. Much detail of rights and wrongs did StoneHouse furnish each Royal with before pronouncing their sentences. The King LightSide suffered the full wrath, and as reward for his unspeakable orders, given in the selfish desire of his being the One Ruler of an entire World, banished was he, to a duplicate of FlatWorld that contained no people and never would. A glimpse did StoneHouse give the King Grey and the White Queen, one look of the burnt and ash-filled realm the White King now ruled from his Black Throne. Desolation there was on his face, and the enormous anger visible was desperate, before the image was ceased, and the White King LightSide was forever gone from the World.

The King Grey he smiled at, compassion and understanding were communicated with only eyes, and sorrow for the pain of his loss were also in the Hansel-figures look. He bade him to take both hands of the White Queen firmly in his both hands and stand facing one another, and in the despite of pains of betrayal and hard loss, to forget about sadness awhile and to set aside grievances. And when they were both embraced in this manner, lo! All grief and hurt seemed to retreat and was replaced with laughter and amazing joy. Green now they were both attired in, and in their own hearts they perceived of the great anxiety dissipating from all houses, and of everything being transformed. And they knew of neighbourhoods across the Lands raising their arms in welcome, singing songs of laughter, and knowing the song echoing from the World they stood upon heralded the return of the Regal Line of King Greenleaf, and days renewed had come.

So the Legend of the Permanent-Peace was come to pass at long last, and was fulfilled as it had been began, by the actions of StoneHouse. And muscular AirSteeds it had provided also, adorned with only saddle, bridle and bit, of functional but comfortable use. Awaiting outside they were, ready to bear the Royals Greenleaf to be with the peoples who would Love and Praise them, and to survey the wondrous GreenWorld that they were both to care for. The panoramic visage from above the few wisps of clouds during the far-journey to the Green City would allow them to fully understand the virtue of GreenWorld, and realise how clearly the Lands would draw Farmers, or lure persons of capable agricultural Husbandry to exploit the blessed merit of such a boon, and to bring impressive yield onto table and plate.

Prior to the Royal King and Queen Greenleaf departing, the image of Hansel bade them approach near. No fear did they feel as they came to be close enough that when Hansel reached out to each of them there was no faltering in their movements in both taking a hold of the very Hand of StoneHouse itself.

A slight thrill of low vibration they could each feel in the grip, and then they felt a wonderful sensation of contentment and sheer joy emanating from Hansel, which they somehow perceived was the mood across the whole realm. And extremely unusual sensations of gratitude there was present also. Puzzled initially, a slow but gradually growing set of memories was awakened in them. Dormant knowledge began to surface and the names of Mac and Mari' were remembered. Then, like the proverbial opening of floodgates, the lives that they had lived previously started to fill their minds, desiring to occupy their respective bodies too. And StoneHouse, and GreenWorld felt this desire growing, and so was executed the Final actions signifying the absolute end of FlatWorld, and the last act of Enchantment that was remained in StoneHouse's sturdy Walls awaited only for the proper moment. When the Royal couple remembered the name of Edinburgh, it happened. Immediately.

(Edinburgh),

Mac and Mari' sat facing each other across the kitchen table, sipping freshly ground coffee. Neither of them spoke aloud for a wee while, being deep in thought. After some time they then talked long of the adventure, as no other word had they for the experience of inter-dimensional travel and living another life. And that way of life and existence was come perilously close to being permanent but for the intuition and interventions of Mari', whom they now comprehended was from the start being helped and directed from afar by StoneHouse, which at long last, in the most recent manifestation of the King Greys Queen, had perceived of the abilities necessary to explicate and translate, then expedite, with an unwavering will and clarity of purpose, the prerequisites for breaking down such a staggeringly prodigious Curse.

Much enjoyment was now felt by them both, and when they had spoken for many hours, they at last had summoned the courage to inspect closely the Chessboard still on the table to the side of them, loosely re-covered with the same blanket used when first they placed the Chess-Set there. No mess of disruption was there, of glass shattered or anything else, when they had found themselves instantly returned to their own dimension with the same ethereal topsy-turvy and floating sensations as when they were departed. The kitchen, and house, was as it had been before the adventure. Even the

Chessboard was closed upon their return, which a thankful Mac for the time being covered over.

With her being marginally nearest, Mari' reached out to lightly grasp the Box, and she slid it directly in front of and between them. Smiling at Mac in the way he adored, she casually discarded the covering and then firmly laid her hand, palm-down on the closed board and indicated that Mac do the same. When he did this with no hesitation in the least, Mari' smiled widely and lovingly at him.

Asking Mac to describe what he was feeling from the Box he frowned, and the instant concerns awakened in his heart for Mari' added to the furrows of his brow. Her twinkle-imbued laughter dispelled these worries, and swept them utterly from his heart. And when she repeated the question, he closed his eyes and considered carefully, his own hand still firm-placed on the Bewitched Box. Mari' silently laughed to herself, watching his concentrated face, with eyes closed becoming more and more amusing as he diligently sought for what was not there. Mac finally relented and opened up his eyes, admitting to his wife that he was given up, and she would have the enjoyment of telling him for what he was searching, as absolutely nothing could he detect. As he uttered these words it dawned on him that the nothingness was what she wants him to find, and what she wants him to feel; removed and gone forever and ever was even the remotest echo of Enchantment or Wizardry.

Leftover, perhaps as Reward valiantly earned, was something to be coveted for all time. An amazingly beautiful, and amazingly created far-Eastern Chessboard of impossible construction. Mac and Mari' exchanged knowing looks, and it required no words to be passed between them for each to be sure that the others thinking was all but identical to their own. Mac was speaking on the telephone, and arrangements were swiftly solidified. Mari' had fetched the Cases that they kept packed should the need or even the urge arise for short-notice travel. Their passports she retrieved also.

(GreenWorld),

The harvest was enormous, with cellars, wine stores and pantries filled to capacity. Delightful were the days and restful and peaceful were the evenings. Songs of cheer and laughter were sung in the Alehouses and Thanksgiving was observed across the realm. The King and Queen Greenleaf were both much loved and they visited extensively of the realm they were to care for and as they went even to remote settlements and isolated lighthouses along any archipelagos, always great praise was given and bestowed upon them.

The Royal Scribes put ink to reams of papyrus, and declared boldly that from the Day of the Permanent Peace onwards the Historical lore of GreenWorld would be recorded and any person who desired as much would be schooled in the arts of written words or of creative artistic expressions of various disciplines. The burdens of the past seemed dreamlike and mothers sang lullabies to babies while fathers attended to work duty or household upkeep. Children ran clamouring and noisy over the green grass, and verily, an Utopian Aura surrounded the entire GreenWorld like a long-lost friend of familiar face and a determined care. Everything was of Light and all hearts were glad, and knew not of hate and distrust of their neighbours.

(City of Kerman, Iran),

Kerman was known for its strong cultural heritage and its long History, even by European reckoning. Mac and Mari' had visited extensively of the many Mosques, but were now approaching the largest and most imposing of the Zoroastrian Fire Temples for speech inside with someone of the greatest importance. They both had spoken years previously to the person mentioned, who was the Prime Representative of the entire Kermanshah Province of the very Ancient area now officially called Iran.

Much mystical sensation there existed, and one need only close their eyes and concentrate on the music arriving on the wind from various unknown distances. The fluted notes of typical Eastern instruments sounded like they brought voices of secrets for the capable to know of, as well as soothing the faithful when they knelt to offer prayer. The other combined noises from the bustling and busy crowded City were as if of respectful background hum, discernible but definitely secondary in nature. And should a person be lucky enough to be gazing upon the Zoroastrian Fire Temple to which Mac and Mari' now approached whilst hearing, feeling almost the rhythms and messages of such musical composition, then fortune, or fate would have indeed turned its smile towards them.

Entering via a seldom-used small doorway into an extremely narrow corridor, there was a lightly robed guide to greet them, bidding that they remove footwear and follow him closely. Many openings large and small they passed, making several turns on their own route before descending an extremely tight and dim spiral staircase. Hopelessly confused to their location a person would easily become if alone and unguided. Miles of passages there were, some leading to places from whence there was no return. Chambers there were where mythological creatures lurked, hoping to snare the unwary or the lost. Mac held clasped firm the soft hand of his Wife and concentrated himself in following the guide, who held aloft only a dim fire-torch, lit from the main Torch of the Temple; a fire that had been giving light unbroken since the dawn of time. A blessed Fire from the very Earth, which the Temple had been built around part by part over ages, like the other Fire-Temples that there existed in only this particular region of the World.

Turning into another corridor, there was an opening into a large and pleasing Chamber, the walls of which were adorned with candles of many flickering colorations, creating a beautifully serene light. The person whom they were travelled to beg audience with was sitting cross-legged on a multi-patterned rug of breath-taking size. He gestured for the couple to sit beside him, and dismissed the guide until he was required once more. Bowing his head, the person they craved speech with spoke aloud, and with surprisingly strong voice declared his welcome of the 'Couple Mackenzie', adding that the passing years were untroubled on the lovely face of Mari', but that more lines were upon the look of Mac, and curious was he to know what Cares were afflicting him, as other senses than sight he possessed. Mac bowed himself in prelude to his own speaking of the events contained in the adventure of GreenWorld. At the mention of that World the person was visibly startled, and begged details of the start through to the ending. Firstly, he insisted that he serve to them Tea, as thirst he had sensed when they were both entered into his personal

Chambers. A place long ages-ago utilised as a hideout and legendary store for Forty Thieves.

Verily, the person they sat with was Ali-baba, known to Mac and Mari' as Aleebba-Ba'Ba, the very same Magician who had schooled Addarra-Cabbaddra, much to his shame and regret, as he knew not he was a Necromancer, who singularly desired only to learn of the power needed in order to enslave whole Worlds, and bend any Mans will to serve only his own wicked purpose. Word of the cursing of GreenWorld had reached the ears of Aleebba-Ba'Ba, as it was the first Great Enchantment AddarraCabbaddra had bestowed since being taught how. Heavy was the sadness in the hearts of many within the multiverse when learning of the fate of such a beautiful World, including Aleebba-Ba'Ba, who had been the Teacher. He sensed that news of balance restored was behind his Visitors purpose, and was gratified beyond the words of happiness at hearing all the details of the adventure of Mac and Mari', and their tiny glimpse of into the might of the multiverse. Water, fresh Tea, and food was brought to them, and a good meeting of Friends long absent was had. When Mari' removed the box she had wrapped up in her backpack and placed it afront of him, it drew out a stunned gasp from the throat of Aleebba-Ba'Ba.

He asked for permission to touch and inspect the box, which was willingly granted. Slow and deliberate were the curious hands and eyes of Aleebba-Ba'Ba as he took some time to look at the box, and the Chess-Set it had stored there within. After a while he declared it to be a creation of his own hand!, constructed by request of the multiverse, and many Enchantments were to bestowed within its parts! He knew not what it was to be used for, but recent events suggested part of

73

that usage involved the concealing of a World, but again he knew not why.

The multiverse answered to no-one but spoke for all; unimaginable in size and age, it continued to monitor infinite trillions of happenings. Minor would be its interest in the Earth dimension and the questions of Aleebba-Ba'Ba, but it would desire the return of the box, of which Mac and Mari', two exceptionally gifted Beings, and the only Humans aware of the multiverse, were both happy to oblige, and so left the box in the safe care of Aleebba-Ba'Ba.

(Edinburgh),

It had been several months now since Mac and Mari' had returned from Iran, and the Summer passing had been unusually warm and sunny. It was a Saturday morning and the Mackenzie's were enjoying their coffee in the garden, a veritable luxury for Edinburgh in late September. Mari' was busy on the laptop checking their business email, whereas Mac had chosen the 'feet up with a newspaper' approach to the weekend. He did stop and lay down his reading when Mari' declared that they had received a communique from the Kermanshah University of Ancient Artifacts. Exchanging one of the knowing glances they had developed over years, they were both aware that the message on the computer had been placed there by the multiverse, as no such institution as Kermanshah UAA had there ever existed.

Mari' skimmed easily through the expected, she supposed, brief and direct email even before Mac was turned to face her to hear what was written to them. As compensation for the return of the box, and the valour displayed on its behalf

and on the behalf of GreenWorld a sum of twenty-five university credits had been credited to their Bank account. Mari' made an exaggerated 'Whooo-ing' sound, but in good humour. Wondering if perhaps that amount would finance a return visit to Kerman, and maybe to other areas that they loved, Mari' clicked on the Finance Icon and scrolled down for a moment, before ceasing where the exchange rate was listed. Mistaking her silence as disappointment, he assured her they'd go back soon, possibly next year, when she burst out laughing and crying and laughing once more. Mari' savoured Macs' befuddled look for a very brief moment, then informed him that one university credit was currently adjusting to around one hundred million pounds sterling! His words as he jumped up and ran into the house sounded like he was asking where Mari' had stored the passports. ***End[1].
***